It Came from Within . . .

The boys turned the corner and screeched to a stop. From across the living room, a tall, hunched-over figure staggered toward them. It looked like a man, but it didn't seem to have any eyes, nose, or mouth.

"What do you want?" asked Oliver, backing up. Matthew was squeezing his arm so hard that Oliver thought he was going to pop a blood vessel.

The figure stretched out its arms. "Lucifer," it said with a hoarse voice. "I came for Lucifer. . . ."

ADVENTURE
IN THE
HAUNTED
HOUSE

ADVENTURE IN THE HAUNTED HOUSE

PAGE McBRIER

Illustrated by Blanche Sims

Troll Associates

Library of Congress Cataloging in Publication Data

McBrier, Page.
    Adventure in the haunted house.

    Summary: While Oliver cat-sits for a vacationing
friend, the cat runs off and gets lost in a haunted
house.
    1. Children's stories, American. [1. Cats—
Fiction] I. Sims, Blanche, ill. II. Title.
PZ7.M4783Ad   1986   [Fic]   85-8436
ISBN 0-8167-0539-9 (lib. bdg.)
ISBN 0-8167-0540-2 (pbk.)

10   9   8   7   6   5   4   3   2

ADVENTURE
IN THE
HAUNTED
HOUSE

5

CHAPTER
1

Br-r-ing. Br-r-ing. Oliver Moffitt, pet-care expert, rolled over in his bed and squinted at the alarm clock. Seven o'clock. Oliver yawned, closed his eyes, and drifted back to sleep. As he slept, Oliver dreamed he was stranded on a desert island like Robinson Crusoe. His only friends were a parrot named Hank and a monkey named Harry. Together they sat on the beach eating mangoes and bananas and speaking strange animal languages.

"Oliver, wake up." Oliver felt someone shaking his shoulder. He opened his eyes slowly. Mrs. Moffitt smiled at him. "You must have been having quite a dream," she said. "I've been calling you from downstairs for ten minutes. Did you forget what day it is?"

Oliver sat up and rubbed his eyes. "Today is Saturday," he said, jumping out of bed, "and I'm getting a new customer."

As owner of a pet-care business, Oliver watched other people's pets. Dog-walking, cat-sitting, and pet-grooming were all part of his job. Oliver was proud of his motto: "I'm good with dogs and good with cats. I'll even baby-sit your rats!"

"What time did you tell Jennifer you would pick up Princess Fluffy?" asked Mrs. Moffitt.

"Eight o'clock," replied Oliver. "I'd better hurry. Her father said he's pulling out of the driveway at eight-fifteen sharp."

Jennifer Hayes was in Oliver's class at Bartlett Woods Elementary School. Her cat, Princess Fluffy, was a beautiful white Persian with dark orange eyes. Jennifer needed a cat-sitter because she was going with her parents to a convention in Florida.

"Lucky Jennifer," said Oliver, pulling on his sweatshirt. "She gets to miss school for one whole week."

"I'd say you're pretty lucky, too," Mrs. Moffitt said. "We've never had a cat before."

"You're right," Oliver agreed. "It should be fun having another pet around."

Oliver lived alone with his mother and her dog, Pom-pom. Oliver's parents were divorced, and his father lived in another city. His mother worked as a bookkeeper at an insurance agency.

"I certainly hope this works out," Mrs. Moffitt said. "I can't imagine keeping a cat here for a week."

"No problem," replied Oliver. "Cats are very easy to care for. All they need is food and water and cat litter. You don't even have to walk them."

Mrs. Moffitt sighed. "Well, I suppose so," she said. "I'm trusting you to do the right thing."

"My pet business is my life," Oliver said. "The only thing we need to do is show Princess Fluffy where her litter box is. The rest is easy. Cats spend most of their time sleeping."

Oliver finished tying his sneakers and headed for the door. "See you soon, Mom," he said.

"Don't forget your jacket," Mrs. Moffitt called after him. "It's chilly this morning."

Oliver ran downstairs, grabbed his coat, and ran out the front door. The air smelled of autumn. Halloween was just a week away. Oliver could see over in the next yard where he and his friend Matthew had helped set up Samantha Lawrence's new pup tent yesterday. Sam was another of Oliver's classmates. Her cat, Achoo, and Princess Fluffy were twin sisters.

In the front yard a pile of leaves moved suspiciously. Out popped Pom-pom's head.

"Come over here," Oliver called. "Were you trying to sneak up on a squirrel?"

"*Yap, yap, yap,*" Pom-pom barked.

Oliver laughed. "You'd better be careful," he said. "You're not much bigger than a squirrel."

Pom-pom was a Shih Tzu, a tiny dog whose ancestors came from China.

"You stay inside," Oliver said. "I'll be back soon with a house guest. You've never met a cat before, have you?" Pom-pom barked happily and ran into the house.

A few minutes later, Jennifer answered the door. She was wearing a Purple Worms sweatshirt and chewing her usual wad of gum. The Purple Worms were her favorite rock group.

"It's about time," she said.

"What do you mean?" asked Oliver.

"You said you'd be here at eight o'clock," said Jennifer. "My watch says 8:03."

"But I *was* here," Oliver protested. "I was walking up the driveway."

Mrs. Hayes came around the corner. "Good morning, Oliver," she said brightly. "Are you here to pick up our little kitty?"

"Yes, I am," he replied.

"Good," she said. "I'm sure Jennifer has told you that we usually board our Princess at Hermann's Pet Palace. However, Jennifer said that you have this new business, and she'd like to give you a try."

Oliver nodded. "I'll take excellent care of Fluffy," he said. "Cats are one of my specialties."

"Come on," Jennifer said, tugging on Oliver's arm. "Princess Fluffy is in my room."

"Be careful not to trip as you run up those stairs," Mrs. Hayes shouted after them.

Jennifer's room was filled with rock-star posters and stuffed animals. The bedspread, rug, and curtains were all purple, Jennifer's favorite color.

"Did you see my newest Purple Worms poster?" asked Jennifer. She pointed at a corner of the wall. "It's a collector's item."

"What's so great about that?" asked Oliver.

Jennifer looked at him in disbelief. "Are you kidding?" she said. "It was taken on the Worms' European tour."

"So?" said Oliver.

"The Worms have never played Europe before," said Jennifer.

Oliver looked around the room. "Where's the cat?"

"Here, Fluffykins," called Jennifer. Princess Fluffy ran out from underneath Jennifer's bed and rubbed up against her leg.

"She looks exactly like Achoo, doesn't she?" said Jennifer.

"Good kitty," said Oliver. Jennifer picked up Princess Fluffy and kissed the top of her head. "This is Oliver," she said. "He's going to take care of you while I'm gone." Jennifer handed the cat to Oliver. "Hold her while I go get the cat case," she said. "She doesn't like this part."

"No problem," replied Oliver.

Oliver scratched Princess Fluffy behind her ears. "You're a good cat, aren't you?" he said. Princess Fluffy squirmed and let out a wail.

"Ow," cried Oliver. "She's digging her claws into me."

Jennifer hurried back into the room. "Here I am," she said. "I'll close the lid if you hold her down inside." Princess Fluffy clawed at Oliver again, but he held her down. Jennifer snapped the lid shut.

"Well, I guess we're ready," Oliver said, looking at his scratches. Princess Fluffy let out another unhappy wail. "Poor Fluffy," he said, peering through the window. "Don't worry. You won't have to stay in there for long."

Jennifer handed Oliver a large shopping bag. "This is Fluffy's litter box, hairbrush, catnip toy, and some food supplies," she said. "She gets a half can morning and night. If you have any problems, call Sam."

From the driveway, Mr. Hayes honked the car horn. "Time to go," said Jennifer. She pressed her lips against the window of the cat case. "Good-bye, my dearest darling cat," she said. "I'll see you next Saturday."

"Yuck," said Oliver. "You sound like a mushy movie."

"Promise you'll take good care of her," said Jennifer.

"No problem," Oliver replied. "What can be so hard about taking care of a little cat?"

CHAPTER
2

Princess Fluffy cried all the way to Oliver's house.

"Mom, I'm home," yelled Oliver as he pushed open the front door.

"What's that terrible racket?" asked Mrs. Moffitt. She was upstairs in her room.

"It's Princess Fluffy. She misses Jennifer," said Oliver.

He carefully placed the cat case on the living-room floor and lifted the lid.

"You can come out now," Oliver said.

Princess Fluffy grew silent. Her orange eyes peered at Oliver.

"Come on out. It's okay," coaxed Oliver.

The cat cautiously put one paw outside her

cat case and sniffed. Slowly, another paw emerged. Then she was out. Princess Fluffy crept across the rug and headed for the sofa.

"Good cat," said Oliver. "Nice kitty."

"*Yap, yap, yap.*" Oliver turned and saw Pom-pom racing across the room toward Princess Fluffy.

"Pom-pom, stop it!" shouted Oliver. "This is not a squirrel."

Princess Fluffy took one look at Pom-pom and puffed up into an enormous fur ball. She let out a bloodcurdling howl and jumped onto the sofa. From there she leaped onto Mrs. Moffitt's antique table.

"Watch out for the plant!" Oliver screamed. Mrs. Moffitt's prized African violet crashed to the floor. Princess Fluffy dashed up the curtains behind the sofa.

"Oh, no!" cried Oliver. There was a loud rip. Princess Fluffy dangled for a moment. At last she pulled herself up to the curtain rod.

"*Yap, yap, yap,*" barked Pom-pom.

"Pom-pom, get off the sofa," said Oliver. Pom-pom looked up at the cat and growled. Princess Fluffy hissed back.

"What in the world is going on?" asked Mrs. Moffitt, coming into the room. She stopped and stared. "Oh, no! My African violet, my curtains!"

Mrs. Moffitt turned to Oliver. "Young man, I hope you're prepared to clean up this mess."

"I'm really sorry, Mom," Oliver replied. "It was an accident. They didn't have a chance to be introduced."

Mrs. Moffitt shook her head. "I just hope this is not a sign of things to come," she said.

Princess Fluffy sat on top of the curtain rod for the rest of the day. Several times Oliver stood on the back of the sofa and tried to coax her down.

"It's okay," Oliver said. "Pom-pom is locked in my room now. You're safe." Princess Fluffy puffed up like a porcupine and hissed at him.

Around suppertime Oliver ran into the kitchen. "Mom," he said, "where's Pom-pom? Princess Fluffy has decided to climb down."

"He's asleep on my bed," said Mrs. Moffitt. "Run upstairs and make sure the door is shut."

Princess Fluffy cautiously sniffed her way through the living room and into the kitchen.

Oliver checked the bedroom door and was back in time to hear his mother say, "Hello, little kitty. Would you like something to drink?"

She pulled a carton of milk out of the refrigerator and poured some into a saucer. Princess Fluffy rubbed up against her leg and purred.

"Hungry, aren't you?" said Mrs. Moffitt.

Upstairs, Pom-pom scratched at Mrs. Moffitt's bedroom door and whined.

"Oliver," said Mrs. Moffitt, "we can't leave poor Pom-pom locked in my bedroom forever."

"You're right," Oliver said. He sat still and thought for a minute. "I know," he said. "Why don't we give Princess Fluffy dinner on the kitchen counter? As long as she knows she's safe, she won't be any trouble."

Mrs. Moffitt frowned. "Are you sure?" she said.

"No problem," Oliver replied. He picked up Princess Fluffy and set her on the counter. "I'll go get Pom-pom."

As soon as Oliver opened the bedroom door, Pom-pom rushed down to the kitchen and began to sniff around.

"Oliver," whispered Mrs. Moffitt, "I don't like this. He's looking for the cat. What's going to happen when they smell each other?"

Princess Fluffy's eyes met Pom-pom's. The two animals froze. With an angry howl, Princess Fluffy vaulted off the counter. A peanut-butter jar crashed into the sink.

"Watch out!" said Mrs. Moffitt. "They're headed up the stairs."

"Pom-pom, Fluffy, come back here!" Oliver yelled. "Stay out of my room. Keep away from that desk." He watched helplessly as Princess Fluffy knocked over his prized stuffed owl and then scattered his math homework across the floor.

With one final, frantic effort, Princess Fluffy squeezed behind Oliver's desk. Pom-pom stuck his nose between the desk and wall as far as he could and barked loudly.

"Where are they? What's going on?" said Mrs. Moffitt, rushing into the room.

"Fluffy's hiding behind my desk," Oliver said.

Mrs. Moffitt paused. "Oliver," she said, "this cat is disrupting our home and it has got to stop. If this keeps up, you are going to have to take her to Hermann's Pet Palace. Do you understand?"

Oliver looked down at the floor. "But Mom," he said, "they're my competition."

Mrs. Moffitt looked at him sternly. "Then you'll have to do a better job," she said. She picked up Pom-pom and held his jaws shut. They went downstairs.

Oliver picked up the phone and dialed. His bedroom was also his office, where he carried on his pet-care service.

"Hello, Sam?" he said. "This is Oliver."

"Hi, Oliver," she replied. "What's up?"

"It's Princess Fluffy," Oliver answered. "She and Pom-pom aren't getting along, and my mom wants to send her to Hermann's Pet Palace."

"That's terrible," said Sam. "Where is Fluffy now?"

"Squeezed behind my desk," Oliver replied.

"She's probably really scared," Sam said. "Cats don't like to be put in strange environments."

"What should I do?" Oliver asked.

"It may take her a while to feel at home," Sam said. "Did Jennifer give you any of her toys?"

"Yes, a catnip sock," Oliver answered.

"Good," said Sam. "Put it near her. It'll make her feel less homesick."

"Okay," Oliver agreed. "I'll put it next to the desk."

"Try leaving some food and water there, too," said Sam. "It may be a few days until she feels like coming out."

"Thanks a lot," Oliver said.

"Good luck," Sam replied.

The next morning, Princess Fluffy was under Oliver's bed.

"Poor Pom-pom," said Mrs. Moffitt. "He kept me up half the night with his whining. I wish he wasn't so distracted by that cat."

"Don't worry, Mom," said Oliver. "By tonight they'll be used to each other."

That afternoon, Mrs. Moffitt stopped by Oliver's room. He was reading the chapter on "Getting Acquainted with Your Cat" in his encyclopedia of pets.

"Oliver," she said, "I'm leaving these piles of folded laundry on your bed. Would you make sure they get put away sometime today?"

"Sure, Mom," said Oliver.

"Where's the cat?"

Oliver sighed and nodded at the bed.

"Maybe she'd like a little luncheon meat," suggested Mrs. Moffitt. "That's one of Pom-pom's favorites."

Oliver looked at his mother. "Thanks, but I don't think so," he said. "People food isn't really good for cats."

Later, Oliver was working in the basement on his Halloween costume when he heard his mother calling him.

"Here I am," Oliver shouted.

Mrs. Moffitt poked her head in the basement doorway.

"What have you done with the laundry?" she asked.

"Sorry, Mom, I didn't get to it yet," said Oliver.

"That's not what I meant," said Mrs. Moffitt. "Maybe you'd better get up here."

Oliver ran to the top of the stairs. In the bathroom, several pairs of Oliver's socks and underwear were scattered across the floor. His Bartlett Woods Tigers shirt was hanging out of the bathtub. Two of Mrs. Moffitt's terry-cloth dish towels lay in the hall. In her bedroom, several pairs of stockings were draped on the bed. Oliver's gym shorts lay on top of Pom-pom's satin pillow.

Oliver walked into his bedroom. The stacks

of sheets and towels had been knocked to the floor.

"Is this your idea of a joke?" Mrs. Moffitt asked.

Oliver scratched his head and looked around the room. "I didn't do this," he said.

"Then who is responsible for this mess?" asked Mrs. Moffitt.

Oliver ran over and peered under the bed.

"The cat?" said Mrs. Moffitt.

Oliver looked up and nodded. "She probably wanted to stake out her new territory," he explained.

"Oliver," said Mrs Moffitt gently, "don't you think we'd all be happier if you took Princess Fluffy to Hermann's Pet Palace?"

Oliver's eyes widened. "No, Mom, please, no!" he said. "She didn't mean it. She's just trying to get used to us."

Mrs. Moffitt sighed and then sat down on the bed. "All right, Oliver, one more chance," she said. "But this is *it*, do you understand?"

Oliver jumped up and gave his mother a hug. "Thanks, Mom," he said. "I promise Princess Fluffy won't cause any more trouble."

Mrs. Moffitt stood up to go. "After you clean up this mess, why don't you take Princess Fluffy for a walk in the park? Pom-pom and I could use some peace and quiet."

"Cats don't go for walks," said Oliver.

Mrs. Moffitt gave him one of her looks.

26

"Okay," he said reluctantly. "I'll put her in my bike basket and take her for a ride."

"Good," said Mrs. Moffitt. "Pom-pom and I will use the time to take a little nap."

Oliver knelt on the floor and peered under the bed. "What do you say, Fluffy?" he said. "How would you like to go to the park with me?"

CHAPTER 3

To get ready for the park, Oliver lined his bicycle basket with a nice, soft towel.

"Mom, have you seen Pom-pom's leash?" he called. "I want to use it on Princess Fluffy."

"You were the last one to have it," said Mrs. Moffitt. "Where did you leave it?"

Oliver searched the house, but the leash never turned up. He went down to the basement and found some string.

"This should hold you," he said, tying the string onto Princess Fluffy's purple collar. "You won't be doing any walking anyway."

Oliver stuck Princess Fluffy in the basket. "Sit," he said. Princess Fluffy let out a howl.

"Once we get going you'll feel better," Oliver said. "Pom-pom loves to ride in here."

Oliver turned up Sutherland Avenue. He was careful to avoid the bumps in the road.

"Much better, huh?" said Oliver. Princess Fluffy squirmed and then seemed to settle down.

At the edge of the park Oliver sped up as he rode past the ice-cream truck. The last time he had been here, he'd been walking an older boy's dog named Bruiser. Bruiser had jumped into the truck and tried to eat all the ice cream. Oliver was still paying for the damage.

Oliver turned left and headed for the duck pond. Soon he could see lots of little children standing at the edge of the pond, clutching pieces of bread. When Oliver was little, he and his mother used to come here all the time.

"Look, Fluffy," said Oliver. "Those ducks are called mallards, coots, and Canada geese." Princess Fluffy sat up.

"Would you like a closer look?" he asked. He carefully lifted the cat out of the basket and put her on the ground. Princess Fluffy crouched low and froze.

"Boo!" said someone behind Oliver.

Oliver jumped and spun around.

"Ha, ha, I scared you," said Rusty Jackson, a sixth-grader at Oliver's school.

"That wasn't funny, Rusty," said Oliver.

Rusty grinned and stuck out his hand. "I'm

sorry, pal," he said. "It was all in fun. Forgive me?"

Oliver shook Rusty's hand reluctantly. Rusty was usually the meanest kid in school. Ever since Oliver had won a bet that Pom-pom could beat Rusty in a bicycle race, Rusty hadn't talked to Oliver.

Rusty pointed at Princess Fluffy. "Where'd you get that white Persian?" he asked.

"How did you know she's a Persian?" asked Oliver.

"My mom has two cats," said Rusty.

"Wow," said Oliver. "That's neat. This is Princess Fluffy. She's a customer."

"She's a nice-looking animal," Rusty said. "How long do you have her for?"

"One week," Oliver replied.

Rusty nodded and smiled. "I know a lot about these cats. If you need any advice, you can call me."

Oliver stared at Rusty.

"What's the matter?" said Rusty.

"You seem different," Oliver replied. "How come you're being so nice?"

Rusty flashed another smile. "Hey," he said, "I'm no sore loser. You won our bet fair and square."

Rusty bent down and scratched Princess Fluffy under the chin. "Good kitty," he said. Rusty climbed back onto his bike. "So long," he said. "Remember what I told you."

"Sure," said Oliver. "Thanks." He watched Rusty ride off and then picked up Princess Fluffy. "I think you've had enough ducks for one day," he said. "Let's go home."

Instead of cutting back through the park, Oliver decided to take the long way. He wanted to give his mother and Pom-pom some more time to rest.

As he headed down Oak Street, past the large, old homes, Oliver felt a slight uneasiness. He usually didn't like to ride his bicycle here because one of the houses was supposed to be haunted.

Oliver pedaled slowly under old, drooping tree branches. A stray cat darted behind a parked car. "This neighborhood doesn't have a single kid," he told Fluffy.

Oliver pedaled faster. "You okay, Fluffy?" he asked. The cat squirmed inside the basket. Just then, Oliver felt a sharp ping on his shoulder.

"Ow! Something hit me," he said. He slowed down to look around. "It must have been an acorn falling from a tree."

Ping. Another acorn hit his spokes. "That's weird," said Oliver. Suddenly, Princess Fluffy let out a howl. The next thing Oliver knew, she had jumped out of the basket. Oliver hadn't tied the string to the handlebars, because the cat had been so calm.

"Hey! Where are you going?" Oliver yelled.

Princess Fluffy took off toward the nearest house.

Oliver threw his bicycle against a hedge. "Stay away from there," he warned.

Princess Fluffy ran past a No Trespassing sign and up a flight of rickety porch steps. The front door was nailed shut, but next to it a window had been left ajar. Princess Fluffy looked up.

"Don't you dare!" shouted Oliver. Just as he reached the porch steps, the cat crouched and jumped. Oliver watched her disappear through the window.

"Oh, no," he said. Oliver's arms dropped to his sides. "Stupid cat," he shouted. "Do you know where you are? You just ran into the haunted house."

Oliver took a deep breath and looked through the window. It was too dark to see anything. "Here, Fluffy," he called. There was no answer. Oliver was just about to crawl through the window when he heard a chilling wail.

"Forget it," said Oliver. "I'm not going in there by myself."

Oliver pedaled home in record time. He knew he had to work fast. Oliver ran upstairs to his office and dialed the phone.

"Hello, Matthew?" he said. "This is Oliver. Are you busy?"

"I'm practicing my karate," Matthew replied.

"This is an emergency," said Oliver. "Can you come over right away?"

"I guess so," said Matthew.

"Thanks," Oliver replied. He slammed down the phone and then dialed again.

Oliver's friend Josh was working on his father's computer. "I'll explain when you get here," said Oliver. "Just hurry, please."

Mrs. Moffitt poked her head inside the bedroom door. "I didn't hear you come in," she said. "Did you have a nice time in the park?"

"We went to the duck pond," Oliver replied. He opened his math homework and pretended to work on a problem.

Mrs. Moffitt looked around the room and smiled. "Well, I'm glad you're back," she said.

Oliver smiled weakly. "Me, too, Mom," he said.

When Matthew and Josh arrived a few minutes later, Oliver led them up to his room and shut the door.

"Princess Fluffy has escaped," he told them in a low voice. "I need you to help me find her."

"Do you know where she is?" Josh asked.

Oliver nodded solemnly. "The haunted house on Oak Street," he replied.

Matthew and Josh looked at each other.

"But it's almost dark," Matthew said.

"Chicken," said Josh. "Do you mean to tell me you believe in ghosts?"

Oliver looked at them both. "You've got to help me," he said. "If I lose Princess Fluffy, I'll never get another customer."

"You're right," Josh agreed.

"Have you got a flashlight?" asked Matthew.

"Sure," said Oliver.

"Then what are we waiting for?" said Josh.

The haunted house looked even bigger than Oliver had remembered. The three boys huddled on the front porch.

"Here's the plan," said Oliver. "Once we get inside, we need to stay together."

"What's that noise?" Matthew interrupted.

"I didn't hear anything," said Josh.

"Me neither," said Oliver. He looked uneasily at the open window. "As I was saying," he continued, "Princess Fluffy will probably be just as scared as we are, so don't expect her to come when we call." He switched on his flashlight. "Let's go."

The boys climbed through the window.

"It sure is creepy in here," said Matthew.

Oliver swung the flashlight around the room. "I heard that a rich old man used to live here. He never had any children or family—just a mean dog named Lucifer. When he died he left the house to Lucifer."

"Then what?" asked Matthew.

"I can't remember," Oliver replied. "Something about the man's ghost."

"Aw, no one really believes that story," said Josh. "There are no such things as ghosts."

"Come on, you guys," said Matthew. "At this rate we'll never find Fluffy."

"Right," said Josh. "I'll look upstairs, and you two stay down here."

"I thought it would be better if we all looked together," said Oliver.

"Forget it," said Josh. "We can cover more ground if we split up." He turned and headed up the stairs.

"No problem," said Oliver. "Princess Fluffy will turn up any minute."

"I'm glad we kept the flashlight," Matthew said.

In the kitchen, a door slammed.

"Josh, is that you?" Matthew called. The two boys walked into the kitchen.

Oliver pointed to a door in the corner. "Look, it was only the wind," he said. Oliver opened the door. "Just a dirty old basement. See, there's nothing down there."

"Shh!" said Matthew. "I heard something." The boys were silent.

"It sounds like someone whistling down there," said Matthew.

Oliver shut the door. "Now I remember," he said. "After the old man died, Lucifer disappeared. He was never found. Not long afterward, the old man's ghost returned. Ever since, he's been walking through the house, whistling for Lucifer."

"Let's get out of here," said Matthew.

"We can't," Oliver replied. "What about Princess Fluffy?"

"Hey, you guys," called Josh. "Come quick. I think I found something."

They dashed to an upstairs bedroom. Josh was holding a small purple object.

"It's Princess Fluffy's collar!" said Oliver. He scanned the room with his flashlight. "She's got to be in here somewhere."

"Maybe Lucifer got her," Josh said, grinning.

"That's not funny," said Matthew.

Oliver was on his hands and knees. "Here, Princess Fluffy," he called. "Time to go home." He stopped and sat up. "Shh. I think I hear her."

There was a faint meow in the distance.

"It's coming from downstairs," said Josh. "Let's go!"

The boys raced back down to the living room.

"This way!" Josh shouted. "It came from around here."

The boys turned the corner and screeched to a stop. From across the living room, a tall, stoop-shouldered figure staggered toward them. It looked like a man, but it didn't seem to have any eyes, nose, or mouth.

"Is this some kind of a joke?" asked Josh.

The figure kept moving toward them.

"What do you want?" asked Oliver, backing up. Matthew was squeezing his arm so hard that Oliver thought he was going to pop a blood vessel.

The figure stretched out its arms. "Lucifer," it said with a hoarse voice. "I came for Lucifer."

The boys turned and ran.

CHAPTER 4

Oliver, Josh, and Matthew pedaled furiously toward Oliver's house. Once there, they collapsed on the front porch.

"I knew it," said Matthew. "It was the old man."

Josh shuddered. "Whatever it was, it sure was creepy."

"Did you see its eyes?" said Oliver. "They were invisible." He shook his head. "Poor Fluffy has to spend the night in there alone with a ghost. We'll never find her now. I'm finished."

"Maybe we can look again tomorrow after school," suggested Josh.

"Right. Ghosts never come out in the daylight," said Matthew.

Oliver thought about the boys' offer. "We can

41

try putting out some cat food," he said. "She would be hungry by then."

"Good idea," said Josh. "That should bring her out."

The boys got up to go.

"Don't worry, Oliver. We'll find her tomorrow when it's daylight," said Josh.

Oliver looked at his friends. "Promise you won't say anything about this at school?"

"We promise," chorused the boys.

After Matthew and Josh left, Oliver sat in the living room and watched *Zoo World* on TV.

Mrs. Moffitt sat down on the sofa next to Oliver. "Did you have fun with Josh and Matthew?" she asked.

"We went for a bike ride," Oliver replied.

Pom-pom hopped onto Mrs. Moffitt's lap and whimpered. "Where's the cat?" Mrs. Moffitt asked suddenly.

Oliver looked at her and hesitated. "She's hiding," he said finally.

Mrs. Moffitt glanced at the curtain rod and then looked up the stairs. "Well, as long as she doesn't decide to sort the laundry again, I guess she's safest under the bed."

Oliver nodded.

The next day at school, Kim Williams, Jennifer's best friend, came up to Oliver.

"How's Princess Fluffy?" she asked.

"Fine," Oliver answered. "No problem."

"Oh, good," said Kim. "I *told* Jennifer that

you'd take better care of Fluffy than Hermann's Pet Palace."

"She's a good cat," Oliver said. He turned and walked quickly to his desk.

During lunch, Oliver, Josh, and Matthew had another meeting.

"I've been thinking," said Josh. He took a big bite out of a hot dog. "We have a bunch of noisemakers at my house left over from last New Year's Eve. Maybe if we walk through the haunted house with them, we can scare Princess Fluffy out of her hiding place."

"And scare away the ghost," Matthew added.

"Good idea," said Oliver. "Why don't I bring Pom-pom along? Maybe he can sniff her out, like a bloodhound."

Oliver finished his milk and stuffed his untouched peas inside the carton. "Anyone else going back for seconds?" he asked. The cafeteria policy was no seconds without a clean plate.

"Me," said Matthew. Matthew always went back for seconds. He was the smallest boy in the class because he'd skipped a grade.

After school, Oliver met Josh and Matthew in front of his house.

"Do we have everything?" he asked. In one hand Oliver carried a plastic bag with Fluffy's food. Under the other arm he held Pom-pom.

"Here, Matthew, try this," said Josh. He gave Matthew a long pink-and-silver paper horn.

43

"That's neat," said Matthew. He blew the horn loudly. "Watch out, old man," he said.

Oliver and Josh laughed. "That's telling him," said Oliver.

The haunted house didn't look nearly as scary in the daylight. It was covered with brown shingles. The glass in several of the windows had been broken, and the shutters hung crazily on rusted hinges. The door and some of the windows were boarded up. In no time, the boys had climbed through the window and were standing in the living room again.

Oliver set a bowl of food on the floor. "No, Pom-pom," he said, pushing the dog away. He looked at Josh and Matthew. "You think six bowls is enough? I'll put three inside and three outside."

"Sure," said Josh.

The boys looked around. Besides the living room, the first floor had a den, a dining room, and a huge kitchen.

"This place is pretty neat in the daytime," said Matthew. "Each room has its own fireplace."

"There must be about five bedrooms upstairs," added Josh. "Wait till you see."

"Let's get started, then," said Oliver. Josh passed out the noisemakers. "We'll search the upstairs first."

The boys and Pom-pom climbed the wide, wooden stairs.

"Here, kitty," Oliver called. "Dinnertime."

Josh and Matthew rattled noisemakers as they ran from room to room opening closet doors.

"Princess Fluffy isn't here," said Oliver finally. "Pom-pom would have picked up a scent by now."

"Why don't you leave another bowl of food up here just in case?" said Josh. "Then we can look downstairs around the kitchen."

Matthew blew his horn in agreement.

Oliver, Matthew, and Josh watched Pom-pom run eagerly back down the stairs.

"Pom-pom isn't usually this excited," Matthew said.

"It's the cat," Oliver replied. "He'd never seen one up close before."

In the kitchen, Pom-pom was about to swallow something.

"I see that," said Oliver. "What have you got in your mouth?" He pushed the dog aside. On the floor was a foil wrapper filled with cat food. "That's weird," said Oliver. "This isn't one of my food bowls."

Pom-pom looked at the cat food and whimpered. Just then there was a loud crash in the basement. The three boys froze.

"Something's down there again," said Oliver.

Pom-pom put his nose to the floor and sniffed his way over to the stairs.

"No, Pom-pom," whispered Oliver. Pom-pom looked back at Oliver and wagged his tail. "Get over here *right now*," demanded Oliver.

Pom-pom peered down the cellar stairs and

started to bark. Before Oliver could grab him, Pom-pom dashed down the stairs.

"Oh, no," Oliver cried.

"What do we do now?" said Matthew.

They could hear Pom-pom barking in the basement.

"Maybe it's Princess Fluffy," said Oliver. "I think we should find out."

"I agree," said Josh. "If you want me to, I'll lead the way." He took a deep breath and then gingerly began to climb down. "Be careful," he said. "These steps are steep and dark."

"I wish we had that flashlight now," said Matthew. He blew his horn.

"Oh, quit acting like a baby," said Josh.

Oliver grasped the wooden railing and tried to see where he was going. "Phew. It smells like a dirty old cave down here," he said. He rattled his noisemaker nervously. "Here, Pom-pom. Where are you?"

As their eyes adjusted to the dim light, the boys could see Pom-pom barking at something in the corner. A shadowy figure stood over him.

"Shoo! Scat!" said the voice. Oliver stopped and grabbed Josh's arm. Standing on an old cinder block was an old, hunched-over woman. She wasn't much taller than Oliver. On her head she wore an old-fashioned hat that looked like a melted Frisbee.

"Is this your dog?" she asked.

"Yes, ma'am," said Oliver.

"Get him out of here," she snapped.

"Here, Pom-pom," called Oliver. Pom-pom looked up at the woman and wagged his tail.

"Scat," said the woman. Pom-pom sat down. The woman looked over at the boys. "You kids don't belong here," she said.

"We're looking for a cat," Matthew replied.

"There are no cats down here," said the woman. "Take your dog and go home."

"What's that noise?" said Oliver.

"Nothing," said the woman.

"But I heard a meow," Oliver said. He walked boldly toward the woman. "I think you have a cat back there," he said.

The old woman flapped her raincoat at him. "Don't be ridiculous," she said.

Oliver ducked and peered around a pile of cinder blocks. "Look!" he said. "Kittens!"

Matthew and Josh came running over. Nestled on some old rags was a big gray cat and four tiny kittens.

"Aw, they're cute," said Matthew.

"But it's not Fluffy," said Oliver. He reached down to pet the mother cat.

"Don't touch them. They're wild," said the woman. Oliver drew his hand back.

"How old are they?" asked Josh.

"They were born this morning," said the woman. "Their eyes aren't open yet."

Oliver picked up Pom-pom. "Why didn't you tell us the truth?" he asked the woman.

"I'm only protecting the cats," she replied.

"But why?" asked Josh. The woman eyed him suspiciously.

"People don't like to see stray cats running around their neighborhoods. They think they carry diseases and dig up gardens and cause trouble."

"Do they?" asked Matthew.

"Sometimes," said the woman. "But the poor little creatures can't help it if they were born without homes."

She looked at Oliver. "Help me down from this, will you?" Oliver gave the Cat Lady his free elbow, and she stepped off the cinder block. Now she was exactly the same size as Oliver.

The Cat Lady looked at the boys again. "Some people try to poison these helpless little cats," she said. "Sometimes they steal them and sell them to laboratories for experiments." She paused and gave them a significant look. "One time I even saw a nasty boy about your age trying to hit one of them with a stone."

"But I'd never do that," Oliver said. "I'm Oliver Moffitt, the pet-care expert."

"Then what are you doing down here?" she asked.

"We're looking for Princess Fluffy," said Oliver. "She's a white Persian that I'm cat-sitting. She was riding in my bike basket, and she got loose and ran into this house."

The Cat Lady looked Oliver up and down. "Haven't seen her," she said.

"But do you think she's around?" he asked.

"Could be. There are lots of stray cats around here. People decide they don't want them and turn them loose."

The Cat Lady reached into one of her long coat pockets and pulled out a foil packet of food. She opened it carefully and placed it next to the mother cat.

"If I were you, I'd paste up some flyers with the cat's description," she said. "Tell people you're offering a reward. It helps."

Oliver groaned. "There go my profits," he said.

"Do you want to find your cat or not?" asked the Cat Lady.

"We can print them ourselves," offered Josh. "That should save some money."

"You're right," said Oliver. "Finding Princess Fluffy is the most important thing."

He offered his business card to the Cat Lady. "If you happen to see a white Persian with orange eyes, please give me a call."

The Cat Lady looked at the card and then stuck it in one of her pockets. "Scoot now," she said. "You're upsetting the kittens."

The boys ran back upstairs.

"What a weird lady," said Josh.

"She looks about two hundred years old," added Matthew.

From inside the living room, the boys heard a voice. "Hello, hello. Anybody home?"

"Someone's on the front porch," Matthew said.

"Come on," said Oliver. "I'd know that voice anywhere."

From the porch, Rusty was peering through the window. "Hi, guys," he said. "What's up? I saw your bikes parked out front."

Before Oliver had a chance to say anything, Matthew opened his big mouth. "We're looking for a cat," he said. Josh poked him in the ribs. "Ow! What did I do?" he asked.

A frown crossed Rusty's face. "You didn't lose that Persian, did you?" he said. "That's terrible."

Oliver looked at Josh and Matthew and then nodded. "Something scared her, and she jumped out of my bike basket," he said. "We've been looking ever since."

"I live near here," said Rusty. "If you want, I can help you look for her."

Oliver hesitated. "Okay," he said finally. "Thanks. Since you're a cat owner, you might as well help."

"Sure," said Rusty.

Josh stepped forward. "Rusty, if anyone finds out that Fluffy is missing, Oliver is out of business," he said. "You have to promise not to tell anyone."

"I promise," said Rusty. "Scout's honor."

By the time Oliver and Pom-pom got home, it was nearly dark. Mrs. Moffitt was in the kitchen fixing dinner.

"I was wondering where you two were," she said. "Did you have a nice day?"

"It was okay," Oliver replied.

"How's the cat?" asked Mrs. Moffitt.

"Fine," Oliver said. He walked to the sink and washed his hands.

"Has she been fed yet?" asked Mrs. Moffitt.

Oliver paused. "Uh, no," he said.

"Good," replied Mrs. Moffitt. "I cooked some liver for Pom-pom's dinner and made extra for the cat." She reached over and picked up a saucer. "Shall I take it up to her?" she asked.

Oliver grabbed the saucer. "No!" he said.

Mrs. Moffitt frowned. "You don't have to grab, Oliver," she said.

Oliver let his hand drop. "I'm sorry, Mom," he said. "Liver is such an excellent source of protein for cats. Let me take it up to her right away. She knows me better."

"All right. If you insist," said Mrs. Moffitt. "But hurry back. Dinner's almost ready."

Oliver ran to his room and shut the door. He looked down at the liver and squeezed his eyes shut. "Here goes," he said. Oliver swallowed the liver in two bites. "Yuck. Disgusting." He placed the empty saucer at the foot of the bed, where his mother could see it, and then stuck his head out the door.

"She loves it, Mom," he called down the stairs.

Oliver closed the door again and tried to think. How was he ever going to find Jennifer's cat in time? He went to the phone and dialed Sam.

CHAPTER
5

Sam sat on Oliver's bed and listened carefully. After he'd finished telling her about the haunted house and the Cat Lady, she leaned back and took a deep breath.

"What can I do?" she asked.

Oliver looked at her and smiled. "After I called you, I had this great idea." He paused. "I was wondering if you would lend me Achoo for a few days." Sam sat forward. "I can't keep Fluffy's disappearance a secret too much longer," continued Oliver. "Besides, if I put my name and phone number on the flyers, everyone will know that I've lost my customer. It's bad for business."

Sam nodded slowly. "You want me to pretend that it's Achoo who's lost?" she said.

"Yes," said Oliver.

"But what if you never find Fluffy?" Sam asked.

"No problem, Sam," said Oliver. "Once we put up the flyers, someone's sure to call. What can be so hard about finding a little cat?"

"I guess I can do it," Sam replied. "But only for a few days. I'll tell my parents that Achoo escaped out the back door."

"Thanks a lot, Sam," said Oliver. "You've saved my business."

An hour later Oliver was sitting at his desk when he heard the screech of a barn owl. He looked at the stuffed owl on his desk. "I know that's not you," he said. Oliver ran to the window and peered out.

"Psst! Oliver!" Sam was standing in the backyard. She held up a bulging pillowcase. "Where do you want her?"

"I thought that was you," said Oliver. "Where did you learn the barn owl?"

"At camp," Sam whispered back. She waved the pillowcase again. "I'll meet you at the back door," she said.

Mrs. Moffitt and Pom-pom were in the living room watching TV. "Hi, Mom. Hi, Pom-pom," said Oliver. He walked quickly through the kitchen and out the back door.

"Here she is," said Sam. She pulled Achoo out of the pillowcase and gave her a big kiss.

"Thanks," said Oliver. "Do you have any special instructions?"

"She likes liver," replied Sam.

Oliver groaned. "I wish she'd been here earlier." He took Achoo in his arms. Sam turned to go. "One more thing," said Oliver. He carefully removed Achoo's red collar and handed it to Sam. "Keep this. I'll put Fluffy's purple collar on Achoo."

"Good idea," said Sam. "Good night, you two."

"Good night, Sam," said Oliver.

Oliver went back and opened the kitchen door. "Good kitty," he said. He gently sat the cat down on the counter.

Pom-pom must have immediately picked up a scent. The next thing Oliver knew, Pom-pom was racing across the kitchen, barking.

"Oh, no," cried Oliver. "Not again." Before anything could happen, he grabbed a couple of glasses off the countertop and stuck them on a shelf.

"Watch out, Achoo," said Oliver. "He'll tear you apart."

Achoo looked down at Pom-pom and flicked her tail. Calmly, she hopped off the counter.

"I warned you," said Oliver.

Pom-pom rushed over to the cat, but Achoo stood still. Pom-pom sniffed her from head to tail.

"Prrrr," said the cat. She arched her back and looked around the room.

"I don't believe this," said Oliver.

"What's going on in here—" Mrs. Moffitt stopped and stared. Pom-pom and Achoo were nuzzling together on the floor. "Well, I'll be," she said. "They've finally made friends, haven't they?"

"Yep," said Oliver. "Finally."

The next morning at school Oliver was filling Josh in on what was happening when Rusty walked up.

"Hi, guys," Rusty said. He put his arm on Oliver's shoulder. "Any news?"

"Not yet," said Oliver. "We're going to put up flyers this afternoon."

"I'll be glad to help," said Rusty.

"You will?" said Josh.

"Sure," Rusty replied. "Why not?"

"We can use you," said Oliver. "Matthew can't come because of his karate lesson. We're meeting at Josh's around three-thirty."

"Sounds good," said Rusty. "I'll be there."

Rusty's friend Jay Goodman walked up. "What are you guys meeting about?" he asked.

"None of your business," said Rusty. "Scram."

Jay gave Rusty a dirty look. "Well, excuse me," he said. "Since when are you friends with fifth-graders anyway?" Jay stomped off.

After Rusty left, Josh pulled Oliver aside. "Oliver," he said, "are you sure about Rusty?"

"What do you mean?" Oliver asked.

"Well, he didn't speak to you for weeks. Now he acts like your best friend."

"It's okay, Josh," Oliver replied. "Rusty apologized. He wants to be my friend."

Josh shook his head. "I hope you're right," he said.

That afternoon, Oliver, Josh, and Rusty worked hard to get all the flyers printed. Oliver came up with the message:

HELP!
LOST CAT.
WHITE PERSIAN
WITH ORANGE EYES.
CALL 555-1183 AND ASK FOR SAM.

REWARD

The boys Scotch-taped the signs on trees on Oak Street and in the park.

"Someone probably thought she was lost and took her in," said Oliver. "We should have her back in no time."

"Yeah," agreed Rusty. "She's probably asleep right now on somebody's lap."

Josh hadn't said much all afternoon. He looked at Rusty and frowned. "Don't be so sure," he said.

"What do you mean by that, Josh?" said Oliver. Josh didn't answer.

As the boys were taping the last sign, Oliver noticed a hunched-over woman pulling a red wagon up the street.

"Look! It's the Cat Lady!" said Oliver. "Maybe she's found Fluffy." The boys ran down the block.

The Cat Lady was sticking a foil packet of food under a bush. Several cats with collars sat on the wagon, surrounded by food supplies.

"Did you find her?" asked Oliver.

The Cat Lady pretended not to hear him. She took another packet from the wagon and shuffled behind the bush. An old yellow tomcat peered at her from across the street.

"I said, did you find her?" repeated Oliver.

The Cat Lady put down the packet and came around to the front of the bush. She looked Oliver right in the eye.

"Is that any way to greet someone?" she asked.

"Sorry," said Oliver. He looked down at the ground. "Hello, ma'am. Did you find her?"

"No, I did not," the Cat Lady said. She returned to what she was doing.

Oliver looked helplessly at Josh and Rusty. "Did you see our signs?" he asked her. The Cat Lady looked at Oliver and nodded. "Well?" he asked.

"Little boys shouldn't have cats," she said. "Maybe you'll find her, maybe you won't." The Cat Lady waved him away. "Go now. I have work to do." Oliver shrugged.

"See you later," he said.

When Oliver got home that evening, Pompom and Achoo were eating dinner side by side on the kitchen floor.

"I can't get over this," said Mrs. Moffitt, beaming. "You'd think it was a different cat."

Oliver smiled weakly. "You sure would," he said. "Did I get any phone calls?"

"No, nothing," said Mrs. Moffitt. "Were you expecting something?"

Oliver sighed. "I guess not," he said.

The next day after school, Sam came running over to Oliver's house.

"You had two calls while we were at school," she said, waving a piece of paper at him.

She and Oliver ran up to his office. With trembling fingers Oliver dialed the first number.

"Mr. Willis, please," he said.

"Speaking," said the voice.

"This is Sam," said Oliver. "I'm calling about my lost Persian."

"Oh, yes," boomed Mr. Willis. "He's a terrific cat. Gray and black with a white mustache. I've been calling him Freddy."

"Freddy!" Oliver shook his head. "Sorry, Mr. Willis," he said. "Thank you for calling, but I'm afraid that's not my cat."

Oliver's next phone call was to a woman with a bubbly voice.

"Did you find your cat yet?" she asked.

"No, ma'am," said Oliver. "Did you?"

"No, no, I wasn't looking," she said. "But, I *do* have a litter of the cutest little kittens you'll ever see. I'm giving them away to good homes, and I thought that since you lost your cat you might—"

"No thanks," Oliver interrupted. "Thank you for calling. But I'd really like to find my cat."

Oliver hung up the phone and looked at Sam. "False alarms," he said. "She's still missing."

The following day was Thursday. Jennifer was due home on Saturday. That afternoon when the phone rang, Oliver jumped six inches.

"Hello!" he shouted. "Oliver Moffitt, pet-care expert."

"Relax, it's me," said Sam.

"Someone called?" asked Oliver.

"Yes," Sam replied. "Mrs. Edna *P-e-t-r-o-s-k-i*," she spelled. She gave Oliver the phone number. "Let me know what happens."

Oliver dialed the number and a little boy answered the phone. "Hi," the boy said. "I have a truck." Oliver could hear a TV blaring in the background.

"Is your mommy home?" asked Oliver. The boy dropped the receiver on the floor. "It's Mommy!" he yelled.

Someone else picked up the receiver. "Mom?" It sounded like a teenage boy.

"Hello. My name is Oliver Moffitt. I'd like to speak to Mrs. Edna Petroski."

"Oh, she's not home," the teenager said. "That's my mom. She's at work."

Oliver's heart sank. "She called about my cat.
. . . It's a white Persian."

"Yeah," said the teenager. "We've got it. She's
white with orange eyes. How much is the reward?" A baby began to cry. "Quiet," yelled the
teenager.

"You do?" said Oliver. He couldn't believe
his good luck. "Ten dollars. What's your ad-
dress? I'll be right over."

As soon as he was finished talking, Oliver
called Sam. "Someone found her," he said. "Let's
go!"

The Petroskis lived in a trailer park on the far
side of town. Sam and Oliver ran up the steps
and rang the doorbell.

A little girl with wild-looking hair and a milk
mustache answered the door. "It's them!" she
screamed. The door slammed shut again.

A moment later the teenager reopened the
door. "Sorry," he said. "Come on in."

Oliver counted five children, including the
teenager. Soda cans and empty potato-chip bags
littered the floor.

"This way," the teenager said. He led Sam
and Oliver back to a tiny bedroom. A baby was
asleep in a crib in one corner. In the other
corner was a cardboard carton.

Oliver rushed forward and peered into the
carton. He sighed and then looked back at Sam.
"It's not her," he said.

"Are you sure?" said Sam.

"Come look."

Sam stared at the cat. "Princess Fluffy is much larger," she said.

The little girl with the milk mustache ran into the room. "Johnny," she said to the teenager, "tell Thomas to stop teasing me."

"You sure this isn't your cat?" Johnny asked Oliver.

"Positive," Oliver replied.

The teenager sighed. "Mom and I found her down in the stadium parking lot. I wanted to use the reward money to help buy a radio. I've been saving for weeks now."

"Maybe someone else has lost her," said Sam. "Try looking in the paper or calling the animal shelter."

Johnny lifted the cat gently out of the box. "She's kind of pretty, isn't she?" he said.

Oliver scratched the cat under the chin. "Yes, she is," he replied sadly. "Too bad she's not Princess Fluffy."

CHAPTER
6

"**O**liver, wake up!" called Mrs. Moffitt from the kitchen. Oliver looked at his alarm clock and groaned. Today was Saturday, the day Jennifer was due home. And it was also Halloween.

Oliver rolled over and buried his head in his pillow. How was he ever going to face Jennifer? What would she say when she found out he'd lost her cat? Oliver squeezed as far as he could under the covers. He wished that he'd never been born.

"Happy Halloween!" said Mrs. Moffitt. She stuck her head in Oliver's door and made a funny sound. Oliver peered out from under the covers. Mrs. Moffitt was wearing his werewolf mask.

"Mom, you look ridiculous," said Oliver. He was in no mood for jokes.

"Wouldn't you like to have a werewolf for a mother?" Mrs. Moffitt teased. Oliver didn't answer.

Mrs. Moffitt took off the mask and placed it over Oliver's stuffed owl. "Did you finish your costume?" she asked.

Oliver shook his head. "It's a stupid idea," he answered.

"Why?" said Mrs. Moffitt. She came over and sat on the edge of the bed. "I think going as an endangered species is a wonderful idea."

"Maybe," said Oliver. "But my costume doesn't look like it's supposed to. Nobody even knows what a caribou is."

Mrs. Moffitt patted Oliver on the arm. "Don't worry," she said. "Those branches make realistic antlers. I'm sure everyone will recognize you."

Pom-pom and Achoo came running into the bedroom.

"How are my little darlings this morning?" cooed Mrs. Moffitt. "Did you sleep well?" The two animals pounced up on the bed and walked on Oliver.

"Hey, watch it," said Oliver crossly. "You're squishing me."

"When is Jennifer due home?" asked Mrs. Moffitt.

"This morning."

Mrs. Moffitt looked at him and smiled. "You're

going to miss Princess Fluffy, aren't you? She's turned out to be a great house guest."

Mrs. Moffitt stood up. "Come on, you two," she said to Pom-pom and Achoo. "I've made sausage and eggs for breakfast." The two animals hopped off the bed and followed Mrs. Moffitt out the door. "Let's go, Oliver," she said. "Breakfast is getting cold."

Oliver rolled over and stuck his head back under the covers. He never wanted to come out. Never.

When his office phone rang one minute later, Oliver pretended not to hear it. He knew it was Jennifer.

"Oliver," shouted Mrs. Moffitt from the kitchen, "are you going to answer that or not?"

"In a minute, Mom," said Oliver. He slowly got out of bed and crossed the room. "Hello?" he said.

For a moment there was silence on the other end. Then a muffled voice said, "Are you missing a white Persian with orange eyes?"

"Yes," Oliver replied slowly. "Who is this?"

"Never mind," said the voice. "Listen." There was a scuffling sound followed by a terrible, screeching meow.

"It's Princess Fluffy!" said Oliver. "I'd know that howl anywhere. Is she all right?"

The voice snapped. "You want your cat back?"

"Of course," Oliver replied. "What's going on?"

"It's not that simple," continued the voice. "Certain terms must be met."

"But I've offered a reward," said Oliver. "How much do you want?"

"I'm not interested in money."

"Then what?"

The voice didn't answer.

"You don't understand," said Oliver. "I have to get that cat back."

The voice snapped again. "Be home at five tonight," it said. "I'll call with more details." *Click.* The phone went dead.

Oliver was too stunned to move. How could this be happening to him? Why would anyone want to catnap Princess Fluffy?

The phone rang a second time.

"Hello!" Oliver said. "Who is it?"

"It's me—Jennifer," squealed the voice. "How's my baby?"

Oliver paused a moment. "Oh, hello, Jennifer," he said finally. "The cat's just fine."

"Good," she replied. "I'll be right over."

Before Oliver could say anything else, she hung up.

Ten minutes later, the doorbell rang. Oliver was eating cold scrambled eggs and sausages. "I'll get it, Mom," he said.

He pushed back his chair and headed for the front door. Truth was the only answer. He would calmly explain the situation to Jennifer and hope that she understood. Oliver took a deep breath and threw open the door.

"Oliver, baby!" said Jennifer. She was wearing a pair of heart-shaped rhinestone sunglasses and a purple-and-gold T-shirt with MIAMI, I LOVE YOU! scrawled on it.

"Jennifer," said Oliver firmly, "there's something we need to talk about."

Pom-pom and Achoo rushed over. "Princess Fluffy!" screamed Jennifer. "It's Mommy!" She picked up Achoo and gave her a bunch of slobbery kisses.

"Jennifer," said Oliver, "we really must talk."

Jennifer wasn't listening. "Let me look at you," she said to Achoo. Oliver grimaced as Jennifer held Achoo high in the air and checked her over. "You look wonderful," she said. "Did you behave for Uncle Oliver?"

Oliver was speechless. How could Jennifer not recognize her own cat?

"Uh, yes," he said slowly. "She got straight A's."

"As usual," said Jennifer. She turned to leave. "Are you going trick-or-treating tonight?" she asked. Oliver nodded. "Good. See you later then."

"Uh, yes," said Oliver. He watched helplessly as Jennifer carried Achoo down the driveway.

As soon as she was out of sight, Oliver raced back to his room. The first person he called was Sam.

"Sam," he said, "something terrible has happened. Jennifer came to pick up Princess Fluffy,

and before I could tell her what happened, she walked off with Achoo."

There was a long silence on the other end. "You gave away my cat?"

"Well, not forever," Oliver replied. He told Sam about the mysterious phone call.

Sam sighed. "Do you have any idea who it might be?"

"Not yet."

"Tell everyone to meet us at the Quick Shoppe in ten minutes," she said. "This is an emergency." Sam hung up.

Oliver felt sick. Now there were *two* missing cats, and it was all his fault.

By the time Oliver got to the Quick Shoppe, Sam had explained to Josh and Matthew what had happened.

"Oliver," said Sam, "we need to get to the bottom of this. Think hard. Do you have any enemies?"

Oliver shook his head. He couldn't think of anyone who was angry at him.

"What about suspicious behavior?" asked Sam. "Has anyone you know been acting weird lately?"

Oliver thought about his mother in the werewolf mask. "No," he said. "Not really."

"What about the Cat Lady?" said Matthew. "She's pretty weird."

"But why would she steal our cat? She loves cats," said Oliver.

"But she doesn't love kids!" said Josh. "Remember when she said that little boys shouldn't have cats?"

"Then why is she offering to give back the cat?" said Oliver.

"Maybe she wants you to promise to take better care of it," said Sam. "After all, you *did* lose her."

"Not on purpose!" cried Oliver.

Kim and her big brother Parnell walked across the parking lot. Parnell was captain of the junior-high football team. He had his pet boa constrictor wrapped around his arm.

"Look, it's Squeeze Me," said Matthew. Everyone ran over to see.

"Careful," said Parnell, "don't startle him." Last year when Parnell was in the eighth grade, he had exhibited Squeeze Me at the Science Fair. According to Parnell's science report, the snake, which was over six feet long, was not poisonous. It ate a live mouse every other week.

"I always wanted a pet snake," said Matthew.

"Me, too," said Josh. "Mom wouldn't let me have one, though."

Parnell smiled. "They're lots of fun," he said. He looked at Matthew. "Want to hold him?"

"Sure!" Matthew replied.

Sam nudged Oliver in the ribs. "Look who just came out of the Quick Shoppe," she said. It was the Cat Lady, carrying two heavy bags. "Matthew," Sam whispered, "you stay here with Kim and Parnell while we investigate. We can't

75

let Kim find out what's going on. She might tell Jennifer."

Oliver, Sam, and Josh rushed over to the Cat Lady. "Let me help you," Oliver said. He took both bags of groceries. They were full of cat food.

"Thank you," the Cat Lady replied. She pointed to her red wagon. "You can put them there."

Oliver watched the Cat Lady carefully.

"Didn't anyone ever tell you it's not polite to stare?" she said.

"Sorry," said Oliver.

"Did you find your cat?" she asked. Oliver looked over at Sam and Josh and then shook his head. "Too bad," she said. "I thought maybe you had. That other boy, the tall one with red hair, just left here with a big bag of kitty litter." She turned and headed up the street.

"No clue there," said Oliver to Sam and Josh.

"Oliver," asked Sam slowly, "what did the Cat Lady mean about that other boy?"

"Oh, she probably meant Rusty," he said. "I tried to call him to come to this meeting, but he wasn't home."

"Didn't the Cat Lady say she just saw Rusty leave here with a bag of kitty litter?" asked Sam.

"So what?" said Oliver. "He has two cats."

Sam's eyes widened. "Since when?" she said. "I've been to his house, and I don't remember any cats."

Josh hit his forehead with his hand. "Of course!" he said. "That's it! Rusty is the perfect suspect. How could anyone so mean suddenly turn so nice?"

"Wait a minute," said Oliver. "What makes you so sure Rusty doesn't have a cat? He could have gotten one recently. When was the last time you were there?"

Sam looked sheepish. "I guess it was a while ago," she replied. "His mother and mine are friends, and when I was in second grade she took me over to play. Rusty was so awful that I made my mother promise we'd never go back."

"Rusty's changed since then," said Oliver, "and he's probably gotten a cat."

"I still think Rusty is a suspect," said Josh.

"Why?" asked Oliver. "He helped us look for the cat. You're just jealous because he and I are friends now."

"That's crazy," Josh shouted. "He was never your friend before this. If you ask me, it was Rusty who stole Princess Fluffy."

Across the street, Matthew, Kim, and Parnell looked up.

"Did I hear someone say Rusty stole Princess Fluffy?" said Kim.

Oliver looked at Josh. "Now you've done it," he said. "Kim's going to blab the whole thing to Jennifer." He gave Josh a shove.

"Ow," yelled Josh. "Leave me alone." He shoved Oliver, and they began to fight.

"You're wrong about Rusty," said Oliver. "You'll see."

"Break it up, you guys," said Matthew. He tried to wedge himself between the two boys, but they kept on fighting. Oliver felt a hand grab his collar.

"Enough is enough," said Parnell. With a powerful tug he separated the boys. "Now what's this about Rusty stealing Princess Fluffy?" he asked.

"It's not true," said Oliver breathlessly.

Parnell sat the two boys down on the curb. "Suppose you tell me what's going on," he said.

Just before five o'clock that evening, Josh, Sam, Matthew, Kim, and Parnell assembled in Oliver's office. Until the problem was solved, Kim had promised not to say anything to Jennifer. And Oliver had promised not to say anything to Rusty. At five sharp the phone rang. Everyone crowded around it.

"Shh!" said Oliver. He cleared his throat and picked up the receiver. "Oliver Moffitt," he answered.

Once again there was silence on the other end.

"Hello?" said Oliver. "Is anyone there?"

"Are you ready for your instructions?" asked the muffled voice.

Oliver breathed a sigh of relief. It was the catnapper. "Yes," he replied. "What would you like me to do?"

The voice whispered, "Do you know where the haunted house is?"

Oliver's fingers tightened around the receiver. "Yes."

"Meet me there tonight at seven-thirty," said the voice.

Oliver remembered the ghost. "But tonight is Halloween," he said. "Are you sure you—"

The voice cut him off. "Do you want your cat back or not?"

"All right." Oliver swallowed hard. "Anything else?"

"Yes," said the voice. "I understand you have a stuffed owl."

"That's right," Oliver said. "I won it at the Science Fair."

"I want that owl," said the voice. "Bring it to me." *Click.* The caller hung up.

Without another word Oliver dialed Rusty's house. Mrs. Jackson answered the phone.

"Hello," said Oliver. "My name is Scott Davis, and I'm selling subscriptions to *Pet World* to raise money for my Boy Scout troop. Are you interested in a one-year subscription to this fine magazine?"

"Thank you, dear," said Mrs. Jackson, "but I really couldn't use it. We don't own any pets."

"Thank you," said Oliver. He placed the receiver back on the hook. "Everything is finally beginning to make sense," he said. "The only person who ever tried to take my owl away was Rusty Jackson."

"That's right," said Sam. "I remember when you bet Rusty that he couldn't beat Pom-pom in a bike race."

"All Rusty wanted if he won was the owl," said Matthew.

Oliver shook his head. "That dirty double-crosser. All this time he pretended he was my friend, just so he could get even. You were right, Josh. I'm sorry I hit you."

"That's okay," said Josh. "You aren't going to let Rusty get away with this, are you?"

"Of course not," Oliver said. "This calls for revenge."

CHAPTER
7

Oliver faced the full-length mirror and frowned. No matter how he adjusted them, his antlers were still lopsided. He took the wire headband off and examined it carefully. It would just have to do.

Being careful not to knock his antlers against the wall, he gingerly made his way down to the living room. "Trick or treat!" he called. Mrs. Moffitt looked up from her newspaper.

"You look great," she said. "Just like a real caribou."

"I'll be back by nine," said Oliver. "I told the other kids I'd meet them down the street."

"Have fun," smiled Mrs. Moffitt. "Try not to fill up on too much candy."

"I won't," said Oliver. He walked through the kitchen and slipped out the back door. Cupping his hands around his mouth, he made an eerie, rasping hiss. "*Kschh, kschh.*"

Several seconds later, he heard the reply. "*Kschh. Kschh.*"

Sam stepped out of the bushes. "Nice work," she whispered. "You sounded like a real barn owl." Sam looked at Oliver. "Are you a tree?" she asked.

"A caribou," he replied. "It's on the endangered species list."

Sam nodded. "Have you got everything?"

Oliver waved a shopping bag. "All set. We're meeting everyone else at the haunted house."

As they walked toward Oak Street, Sam and Oliver talked.

"I still can't believe Rusty did this," said Oliver. "After everyone left, I started thinking. He must have followed me that day I ran into him in the park. I thought a falling acorn startled Fluffy, but now I realize it was probably a well-aimed stone."

Sam grabbed his arm. "And the ghost?" she asked.

Oliver shook his head. "Rusty had us all fooled."

When they got to the park, Sam and Oliver grew quiet again.

"It sure is empty in here," said Sam. The

playground jungle gym sat like a sleeping mechanical beast. The ducks were all asleep, too.

As they neared the other side of the park, Sam and Oliver could see a rapidly approaching figure.

"Psst! Sam! Oliver!" A short werewolf came running toward them.

"Is that you, Matthew?" asked Oliver.

Matthew took off his mask. "How'd you know?" he asked. He waved his flashlight at Oliver. "What are you? A moose?"

"A caribou," Oliver replied. "Same family, different species."

Matthew nodded. "I hope we get this over with fast," he said. "I have lots of trick-or-treating to do." He spun around and gave a karate kick.

"That looks like Josh, Kim, and Parnell up ahead," said Sam.

Josh had on a white coat and a funny pair of glasses with dangling eyeballs. "I'm a mad scientist," he said, waving a test tube. "Like Dr. Frankenstein."

Oliver looked at Kim. "You must be Frankenstein's monster."

"I'm a rock star."

"Sorry." Oliver glanced nervously at his watch. Rusty was probably already inside the haunted house.

"Hey, Rudolph, let's get this show on the

road," interrupted Parnell. "I have a party to get to."

"I'm a caribou, not a reindeer," Oliver replied. He noticed Parnell wasn't wearing a costume.

"Sorry," said Parnell.

Oliver cleared his throat. "Do we have everything?" he asked. Kim held up a shopping bag exactly like Oliver's.

"Good," said Oliver. "Before we go inside I have some good news. I have reason to believe that the ghost we saw in there is not really a ghost."

Matthew's eyes widened. "You mean . . ."

"We'll just stick to our plan, okay?" said Oliver. Everyone nodded.

Several minutes later Oliver crawled through the living-room window. "The shopping bags," he whispered to Kim. She leaned out and took them from Parnell, who waited outside.

Soon everyone was clustered in the center of the living room. Oliver looked at his watch again. "Any minute," he said. Matthew lowered his mask.

There was a scuffling sound upstairs, followed by footsteps. Someone was coming down the stairs.

Matthew flipped his flashlight on. "Turn it off," whispered Oliver.

Clump, clump, clump. Oliver held the shopping bag tightly and faced the hallway.

"I hope this is who we think it is," whispered Sam.

There was a long, soft whistle. A shadow lengthened against the wall.

"Here he comes," whispered Josh.

"Poor Lucifer," moaned the ghost. He staggered toward the group.

"What do you want?" demanded Oliver.

"If I can't have Lucifer, I want that owl," he moaned.

Sam nudged Oliver in the ribs.

"It's right there," Oliver pointed.

"Prove it," said the ghost.

Oliver walked over and pulled the owl out of the shopping bag. "There!" he said. He put the owl back in the bag. "Now what will you give me in exchange?"

The ghost reached under his huge coat and pulled Princess Fluffy out by the scruff of her neck. She hissed angrily. The ghost dropped her on the floor.

"Here, Fluffy," called Oliver. The cat ran over to him.

"Get ready," Sam whispered to Kim. During all the commotion, the others had quietly moved in front of the shopping bag. Josh and Matthew quickly switched bags.

"Here's the owl," Josh said. He slid the second shopping bag to the middle of the floor.

"Mine!" shouted the ghost. He greedily

shoved his hand into the bag to pull out the owl.

The ghost looked down and screamed. Writhing in his hands was Parnell's boa constrictor, Squeeze Me. The snake bared its fangs and hissed menacingly.

The ghost threw his hat on the ground and ripped a stocking off his face. It was Rusty. "Help!" he screamed. "It's attacking me!" Squeeze Me slid out of the shopping bag and wrapped itself around Rusty's leg.

"Help!" Rusty screamed again. "Get off me!" Rusty threw off his coat next, revealing football shoulder pads and elevator shoes.

He tried to unwrap the snake from his leg. "Do something!" he yelled, backing up against the wall. No one moved. Rusty looked around the room desperately. Squeeze Me unwrapped itself from Rusty's leg. Without looking back, Rusty climbed out the living-room window and ran off.

"Mission accomplished," said Oliver. His friends let out cheers.

"Good work," said Sam.

"I wasn't scared for a minute," added Matthew.

"How are you going to switch cats?" Kim asked.

"No problem," replied Oliver. "Sam and I already have a plan, don't we?"

"We'll do it tomorrow," Sam said. "Right now, though, I'm starving. Why don't we go trick-or-treating?"

CHAPTER
8

The next afternoon Sam and Oliver gave Jennifer a call.

"Hi, Jennifer," said Oliver. "How's the cat doing?"

"She must have really liked your house," Jennifer replied. "Ever since she's been back, she's been acting like a stranger."

"I'm sure she just needs a few days to get adjusted," Oliver said. "How about if Sam and I bring Achoo and Pom-pom over to play? That should cheer her up."

"Good idea," said Jennifer. "We can have a pet party. I'll make little snacks for the animals and we can eat Halloween candy."

Oliver made a face. "We'll be over soon," he said.

Jennifer answered the door wearing shorts and her Miami T-shirt.

"Aren't you freezing?" said Oliver. He took off his jacket and rubbed his hands together.

"The tanner you are, the warmer you stay," said Jennifer.

Pom-pom pulled on his leash.

"You can let him loose if you want," said Jennifer. "My mom doesn't care."

"I prefer to keep him with me," Oliver answered. All the way over, Sam had carefully carried Princess Fluffy's cat case with the window facing away from Pom-pom. So far Pom-pom hadn't paid any attention to her.

Sam looked around anxiously. "Where's your cat?" she said.

"Probably on my bed," Jennifer replied. "She used to never sleep there, but now she loves it."

Sam nudged Oliver in the ribs. "Oliver," she said, "why don't Pom-pom and I help Jennifer make pet snacks in the kitchen while you take Achoo back to play with Princess Fluffy?"

"Good idea," said Oliver. He secretly gave Sam a thumbs-up sign.

In Jennifer's bedroom, Achoo looked at Oliver and lazily stretched her paws. Oliver gave her a nice, long scratch behind the ears.

"*Mew*," squeaked Princess Fluffy from her cat case.

"I'll get to you in a minute," said Oliver.

He carefully removed the purple collar from Achoo.

"Now it's your turn," he said to Princess Fluffy. Off came Achoo's red collar. "No problem," said Oliver. "Now all I have to do is put the right collar on the right cat."

Oliver reached for Princess Fluffy, but before he could grab her, she started to chase Achoo around the room.

"Come back here," Oliver yelled. The cats ran under the bed, behind the dresser, and across the desk. "Oh, no," cried Oliver. "I'm not sure now which is which!"

"Party's on!" Jennifer called from the kitchen.

"Coming!" Oliver replied. He ran over and slammed the bedroom door. "Here, Fluffy," he called. Both cats darted out of the closet. Oliver closed his eyes. "Eenie, meenie, minie, mo." He grabbed the first cat that ran by.

"What's keeping you?" Jennifer yelled again.

Oliver quickly fastened the purple collar on the cat. "I hope I'm right," he said to himself. Just as he got the second collar buckled, Jennifer opened the bedroom door.

"Snack time, Fluffy," she said. She picked up the cat with the purple collar and headed for the kitchen.

Oliver crossed his fingers and waited. He heard Jennifer scream in the kitchen.

"Fluffy, stop clawing me!" she yelled. "It's only a little dog."

Oliver smiled. "Here Pom-pom," he called. Pom-pom ran into the bedroom and up to Achoo.

The cat purred. Pom-pom wagged his tail.

Sam stuck her head in the door. "Everything okay?" she whispered.

"No problem, Sam," said Oliver. "I can't think of a more purr-fect ending to this job."